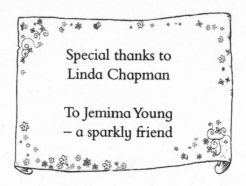

Special thanks to
Linda Chapman

To Jemima Young
– a sparkly friend

ORCHARD BOOKS

First published in Great Britain in 2013 by Orchard Books
This edition published in 2017 by The Watts Publishing Group

9

© 2013 Hothouse Fiction Limited
Illustrations © Orchard Books 2013

The moral rights of the author and illustrator have been asserted.

A CIP catalogue record for this book is available from the British Library.

ISBN 978 1 40832 379 3

Printed in Great Britain by Clays Ltd, Elcograf S.p.A.

MIX
Paper from
responsible sources
FSC® C104740

The paper and board used in this book are made from wood from responsible sources

Orchard Books
An imprint of Hachette Children's Group
Part of The Watts Publishing Group Limited
Carmelite House, 50 Victoria Embankment, London EC4Y 0DZ

An Hachette UK Company
www.hachette.co.uk
www.hachettechildrens.co.uk

Series created by Hothouse Fiction
www.hothousefiction.com

Lily Pad Lake

ROSIE BANKS

ORCHARD

The Secret Kingdom

Lily Pad Lake

Contents

Honeyvale
Swimming Pool

"Watch this!" Jasmine called to her best friends, Ellie and Summer, as she stood on the side of Honeyvale Swimming Pool. She dived perfectly into the deep water, barely making a ripple in the smooth blue surface.

"Oh, I wish I was brave enough to dive like that," Summer sighed.

"That was brilliant, Jasmine!" Ellie clapped as Jasmine bobbed up with her long dark hair clinging to her back and a big grin on her face. "My turn now."

Jasmine swam over to watch with Summer as Ellie got out of the pool. Jasmine's grandma waved and smiled at them from the café.

"Geronimo!" Ellie cried, jumping into the air in a star shape and pulling a funny face before plunging down into the water in a tangle of arms and legs.

Summer and Jasmine giggled as droplets of water splashed them.

Ellie surfaced next to them, her green eyes dancing and her usually curly red hair plastered against her head. "At least I didn't do a belly flop," she giggled.

"You try now, Summer," said Jasmine.

"Um..." Summer hesitated. "I don't really like diving and jumping in. The water always gets up my nose."

"Go on, Summer," Ellie urged her. "It's really fun."

Butterflies fluttered in Summer's stomach at the thought and she shook her head.

"It's all right, you don't have to," Jasmine said, seeing her anxious face. "Let's all play chase instead."

"Can we play in the shallow end?" Summer asked hopefully.

Jasmine nodded. "Of course."

"I'm not it!" cried Ellie, speeding off through the water.

"I will be," said Jasmine. "I'll count to ten. One, two, three…"

Summer splashed away, but even with a head start it didn't take Jasmine long to tag her.

"Got you," Jasmine gasped, touching her arm.

"You're too fast!" Summer laughed.

"Okay, I'll get Ellie instead." Jasmine set off.

Summer smiled as she watched Jasmine chase Ellie across the pool and dabbled her fingers in the rippling water. She liked swimming but she wished she didn't feel so worried about going out of her depth.

It was so much easier when we were swimming with the mermaids in the

Secret Kingdom, she thought to herself. Then she'd been sprinkled with magical bubble dust that had let her breathe underwater.

The Secret Kingdom was a wonderful land that only she, Ellie and Jasmine

knew about, where amazing creatures
like unicorns, elves and pixies lived.
Summer, Ellie and Jasmine had first
discovered it when they had found a
magic box at their school jumble sale,
and since then they'd had all sorts of
adventures there. Their pixie friend
Trixibelle sent them a message in
the Magic Box whenever the Secret
Kingdom needed their help.

Summer knew there was trouble in the
enchanted land at the moment. King
Merry, the happy king, had been given
a cursed cake by his sister, evil Queen
Malice. She wanted to become the ruler
of the land and so she had poisoned the
cake with a curse that was slowly turning
King Merry into a horrible creature
called a stink toad. If King Merry didn't

drink a counter-potion by the time of the Secret Kingdom's Summer Ball he would be a stink toad for good! Summer, Ellie and Jasmine had promised to help find the ingredients to make the counter-potion. So far they had managed to collect bubblebee honeycomb, silverspun sugar and dream dust, but there were still three more ingredients to find, and time was running out.

Summer glanced towards the changing rooms. She and her friends had started taking the Magic Box everywhere with them so that they wouldn't miss a message from the Secret Kingdom. They had left it in Jasmine's bag in their locker while they were swimming. What if their friends in the Secret Kingdom needed them right now? *I'll just go and check it,*

Summer thought, pulling herself out of the pool.

The others swam over as they saw their friend get out. "Are you okay, Summer?" Ellie asked.

"Yes," Summer replied. "I'm just going to our locker to have a quick look."

Ellie and Jasmine smiled. They didn't need her to say any more, they knew *exactly* what she meant.

"We'll come with you," Jasmine grinned.

The three girls hurried to the changing room, dripping water as they went.

When they reached their locker they stopped. A light was shining out around the edges of the locker door!

"The Magic Box!" gasped Jasmine. "It's glowing!"

Ellie looked round. Luckily there was
no one else in the changing room to see.
"Quick. Let's get it out and see if it has a
riddle for us!"

Jasmine unlocked the locker and pulled
out the beautiful carved wooden
box. Shining words
were already
forming in the
mirror
on its lid.

"There *is*
a message!
We've got
to find
somewhere
safe to
read it." she
exclaimed.

Summer had an idea. "What about one of the cubicles?"

It was a squeeze to get all three of them inside a cubicle but they just about managed it. The girls all stared at the lid as Summer read out the words:

"The next ingredient is found
Where water splashes to the ground.
Go to a lake with floating flowers
Where nymphs all play for hours
and hours."

As she finished reading, the Magic Box burst open and an enchanted map of the Secret Kingdom flew out of it in a blaze of light. The map unfolded itself in front of their eyes, showing the whole of the colourful crescent-shaped island just as

if the girls were looking down at it
through a window. The bakery elves were
bustling around at Sugarsweet Bakery,
flags were flying at the top of the turrets

of the pink Enchanted Palace, and on rocks in the aquamarine sea, beautiful mermaids were combing their long hair.

"I wonder where we have to go this time?" Jasmine said, her brown eyes scanning the map.

"Somewhere there's a lake," said Ellie in a low voice so no one outside the cubicle would hear.

"And nymphs and flowers..." added Summer.

"Look! Here!" Jasmine exclaimed.

"Sssh!" Ellie said quickly.

Jasmine pointed to a silver lake
surrounded by waterfalls that cascaded
down from the cliffs
high above it.
Little figures
were
swimming
in the
water
and there
were huge
white
water lilies
dotted all
over it. "Lily Pad
Lake," she whispered,
reading out the label on the map.

"That must be where we need to go,"
Ellie said in delight. The girls grinned

at each other in excitement. Another adventure was about to begin!

Lily Pad Lake

The three girls placed their hands carefully on the Magic Box's shining jewels. "The place we have to go is Lily Pad Lake!" they chorused.

Suddenly a stream of pink sparkles exploded out of the lid of the box, filling the changing cubicle. The girls blinked as they saw their friend Trixi, the royal pixie,

appear, spinning round and round as she
shot all the way up to the ceiling on her
floating leaf. She swerved just in time and
swooped back down towards them.

"Hello, girls," Trixi gasped. She stopped
her leaf in front of their noses and
grinned at them. She was wearing a
pink and white knee-
length dress with
lots of diamond-
shaped jewels
sewn around
the bottom.
Her messy
blonde hair
stuck out
in every
direction,
covering her

pointy ears. "It's so lovely to see you all again!"

"And you, Trixi," Summer whispered, putting out her hand for the little pixie to balance on.

Trixi flew her leaf down and landed on Summer's hand as lightly as a butterfly. "Where are we? And why are you whispering?" she asked, looking around.

"We're in a swimming pool changing cubicle," Jasmine explained. "And we're whispering because we don't want anyone to hear us. My gran might come looking for us at any minute."

"Has your Aunt Maybelle discovered what ingredient we need to find next for the counter-potion?" Ellie asked eagerly. "Is that why you sent us a message?"

Trixi's aunt was a very wise old pixie.

She was working out exactly what they needed to put into the counter-potion to cure King Merry.

Trixi nodded. "Yes. We have to collect some healing water from one of the waterfalls around Lily Pad Lake."

Ellie looked at their swimming costumes. "At least we're dressed for visiting a lake!" she giggled.

"You are!" Trixi smiled. "And I should be too." She tapped her pixie ring and instantly her dress changed into a white halter-neck swimming costume with a short pink skirt over it. Glittery flip-flops appeared on her feet, and a white swimming cap decorated with pretty pink flowers covered her hair. She grinned at the girls and chanted:

"Good friends fly to stop the curse
Before King Merry gets much worse!"

A golden cloud whirled through the
cubicle. It surrounded the girls in a
glowing haze. They grabbed one another's
hands just as they felt themselves being
lifted up and spun away.

After a few seconds, the magic gently
set them down. The whirlwind faded
and the girls gasped. They were standing
beside the beautiful lake they had seen
on the map! At the edge of the lake the
water was so clear that they could see
down to the bottom, where little crystal
stones glittered. All around the lake,
waterfalls were cascading and splashing
down into the water, sending up sparkles
of light.

"Which waterfall do we need?" Jasmine
asked.

"I don't know," Trixi said, looking round
at all the tumbling water. "It's called
Clearsplash Waterfall, but I don't know
which one that is."

"Can we ask them?" Summer suggested,
pointing at a group of boys and girls

playing in the water. They were all tall
and slender with pale blue skin, silver hair
and large eyes like the bluest rock pools.
Some of them were riding around on
giant water snails.

"Who are they?" Ellie gasped.

"They're the water nymphs," giggled Trixi. "Don't you have water nymphs in the Other Realm?"

"No!" Jasmine smiled, her brown eyes wide.

"They're beautiful," breathed Summer.

The water nymphs were wearing long dresses and shorts made out of riverweed. They were having such fun swimming and riding the snails that they didn't notice Ellie, Summer, Jasmine and Trixi watching them.

"They're like merpeople, but they have legs, not tails," Trixi explained. "They live underwater most of the time but they can breathe air too."

Jasmine couldn't wait any longer. She called to the water nymphs. "Hello!"

she cried, cupping her hands round her
mouth to make her voice travel further.

The water nymphs turned and stared.
The next second, they and their water
snails had all dived into the lake and
disappeared!

"Oh, no," said Jasmine in disappointment. "What did I do?"

"It's not your fault," Trixi explained. "Water nymphs are very shy, and they must have been too far away to see your tiaras."

Ellie reached up and touched her golden tiara. Whenever the girls arrived in the Secret Kingdom, special tiaras appeared on their heads so that everyone they met would know that they were there to help King Merry.

Ellie looked round at all the waterfalls. "I hope they come back soon. We have to ask them which one Clearsplash Waterfall is."

"Maybe I can dive down and get their attention?" Jasmine suggested, dipping her toes in. The lake was deliciously warm, just like a bath. "I'm going in!" she said.

"Me too!" Ellie cried.

"Wait," Trixi said to the girls. "You don't want to risk your tiaras falling off while you're in the water." She tapped her ring and chanted:

"Whatever happens, tiaras stick fast
Until my friends complete their task."

"Thank you," grinned Jasmine. She'd hate to lose her beautiful tiara.

"I'll be there in a second." Summer said. She'd noticed something a little way off. One of the giant snails was tied up and had been left behind when the others dived underwater. His horns were wiggling in alarm as he tried to break free. "Oh, poor thing." Summer's heart went out to the scared creature. She loved all animals and hated to see them upset or frightened. "I'll let him go and then I'll join you," she called to the others.

She ran around the edge of the lake. As she got closer the snail panicked even more and tucked his head inside his shell.

"It's all right," Summer soothed him. "I'm not going to hurt you. I'm just going to untie you so you can find your friends."

The snail's head crept out of his shell. His eye stalks waggled uncertainly.

"That's it. There's really no need to be afraid. I just want to help you," Summer said softly. Now she was closer to him she could see the beautiful spiral pattern on his purple shell. "You're so gorgeous." She unhooked his reins from the plant stem they were tangled in, and the snail dived happily into the water.

"Thank you for helping him," a voice said shyly.

Summer jumped and looked round.

A girl water nymph was peeping at her from behind some nearby reeds!

Making Friends

"The snail's name is Curly," the water nymph girl said to Summer as the snail swam over to her and nuzzled her shoulder with his nose. "Because of the curl on his shell." She traced it with her fingers.

"Is he yours?" Summer asked.

The water nymph nodded and swam out from behind the reeds.

"You're really lucky," said Summer.

The girl smiled at her shyly. "Would you like to stroke him?"

"Yes please!" Summer replied enthusiastically.

"My name's Nadia," the nymph told her. "What's yours?"

"I'm Summer," Summer replied. She waded into the water and swam over to Curly. Nadia was rubbing his neck. Summer stroked his smooth shell and he nudged his head against her hand, making her giggle.

Nadia gasped as she noticed Summer's tiara. "You must be a visitor from the Other Realm!" she said. "Are you one of the human girls who has been helping to stop Queen Malice?"

Summer nodded. "My friends, Ellie and Jasmine, are over there." She glanced round to where the others were. "They're trying to dive down and talk to some of the nymphs." As she watched, Ellie came to the surface with a splash and Trixi dodged out of the way of the spray.

"They'd never be able to dive deep enough," Nadia told her. "And it doesn't matter, since you've found me now! So why are you here at Lily Pad Lake?" she continued.

"We need to get some healing water from Clearsplash Waterfall. Oh, please can you tell us which one it is?"

"It's that one, right over there." Nadia pointed at the waterfall at the farthest side of the lake. Summer's shoulders sagged. It would take them ages to walk all the way round the lake.

"We have to get there as soon as we can," she told Nadia, and explained what Queen Malice had done to King Merry. She bit her lip. "The thing is, King Merry doesn't actually know he's turning into a stink toad. The pixies cast a forgetting spell on him and we're trying to get the ingredients for the counter-potion and get him to drink it before he realises. But we've got to hurry. If he doesn't drink the counter-potion by midnight on the night of the Summer Ball, he'll be stuck as a stink toad forever!"

"Oh, dear!" Nadia's eyes grew wide and her pretty face creased with worry. "King Merry is so lovely! Would you like me and my friends to help you get to the waterfall as quickly as possible?"

"Yes, please!" said Summer.

"I'll go and get them." Nadia leaped onto Curly's back and they disappeared down into the depths of the lake.

Summer rushed back to the others.

Ellie waved as she got closer. "Clever Summer, you found a water nymph!"

"Yes – and she told me which one the waterfall is!" Summer cried. "She's really friendly." Her eyes shone. "She's called Nadia and she's coming back with all her friends. They're going to help us get to the waterfall."

As she spoke, one blue head and then another popped up. "Look!" said Summer in delight. Suddenly all the water nymphs were there. Now they knew that Summer, Ellie and Jasmine were friendly, they waved and swam over to the girls.

When Nadia reached them, Summer

introduced her to the others. "This is Ellie and Jasmine – and Trixi. She's a royal pixie!"

Trixi swooped down on her leaf. "It's lovely to meet you, Nadia."

"Summer's told me why you are here," said Nadia. "We want to help King Merry. We've brought our water snails – if you ride on their backs they'll get you to Clearsplash Waterfall as quickly as they can."

"Oh, thank you!" cried Summer, Ellie and Jasmine in delight.

Three of Nadia's friends led Curly and two other giant water snails over. Their horns waggled in a friendly way. Each of the snails had a golden bridle with long reins. The snails sank down in the water so that the girls could scramble onto their smooth, polished shells. Once everyone was on, the snails began to glide through the water. Ellie was glad that she had the reins to hold onto – otherwise she was sure she'd slip off into the lake!

"This is so cool," gasped Jasmine, patting her snail on his smooth neck as he started to swim towards the waterfall, guided by one of the water nymphs.

"It's amazing," said Summer, stroking Curly's shell. He waved his eye stalks happily. They were in deep water now but she didn't feel scared at all with so many friendly water nymphs around her and Curly swimming so smoothly beneath her.

"I never thought I'd be riding a giant water snail today," grinned Jasmine.

"I never thought I'd *ever* ride a giant water snail!" laughed Ellie.

The snails swam towards the waterfall as fast as they could, dodging round the clumps of lily pads that were spread out like green stepping stones on the water.

"That's Clearsplash Waterfall ahead," said Nadia, pointing to a waterfall in front of them. As they drew closer, they could see that the water was spilling down from a sparkling cave right at the top of the cliff.

"Look, there are elves over there, drinking the water," Jasmine called.

"And pixies too," cried Ellie, spotting a group of pixies who were hovering their leaves next to the waterfall as they filled up their little acorn cups.

"Are they all here so that the water can heal them?" Jasmine wondered out loud.

"Yes," Nadia told her. "The healing powers of the water from Clearsplash

Waterfall are known throughout the kingdom. It can make anyone better. We think it's because the water filters through the layers of crystal in that cave at the top of the cliff. If people are unwell they come here and drink some of the water. The waterfall pixies help by fetching it."

"Well, I might not be a waterfall pixie, but I'm going to collect some for King Merry's potion," said Trixi, tapping her ring and magicking a little crystal bottle out of the air. She swooped away on her leaf.

"As soon as Trixi's got the water, we'll have another ingredient to add to the counter-potion," Jasmine said happily.

But just as she spoke there was a disturbance at the waterfall. All the elves scattered, and the pixies flew their leaves away. Trixi zoomed back to the girls without getting any water at all.

"What's happening?" gasped Nadia fearfully.

Ellie looked round and noticed that all the other water nymphs were staring at something in the sky. They were pointing

and shouting. She gazed up and an icy
chill ran through her.

A giant black heron with red eyes and a razor-sharp beak was swooping straight towards them. On his back was the bony, wild-haired figure of King Merry's sister – evil Queen Malice!

A Wicked Spell

Queen Malice's dark eyes glittered
and she shook her spiky black staff
menacingly as the heron swooped over
the lake. Behind it flew five of Queen
Malice's Storm Sprite servants. Their
leathery wings flapped and they had
mean expressions on their pointed faces.

They cackled as the water nymphs shrieked in fear and disappeared into the lake. The water snails followed them.

"Jump off!" Jasmine yelled to Ellie and Summer as their water snails dived underwater. "We can't let Queen Malice get to the waterfall. Who knows what she'll do to it!"

They slid off the snails' backs into the water and swam towards the waterfall. The queen's heron glided down and landed on the nearby shore. The elves and pixies all fled, hiding behind bushes and rocks.

The lake was now empty apart from the girls, who were treading water as Trixi flew anxiously above their heads on her leaf.

Queen Malice glared around at the

pixies and elves peeping out at her. "I heard you – playing with your friends, laughing, enjoying yourselves, drinking the water. Having *fun* together!" She spat the words out. "Well, not any more.

You won't be having any fun when my stupid brother's a stink toad and I rule the Secret Kingdom. I'll stop the waterfall and then you'll never get the healing water you need for the counter-potion!"

"No, you won't!" Jasmine shouted furiously. "We won't let you!"

The queen threw her head back and shrieked with laughter. "What? You three silly human girls really think you can defeat *my* magic?"

"Yes!" cried Ellie. "We've beaten you before!"

"Well, not this time," snapped the queen.

"Why do you have to be so horrible?" Jasmine burst out. "Why can't you just let people be happy?"

"Why should everyone else be happy

when I'm not?" snarled Queen Malice. "Now…" She raised her spiky staff menacingly.

"No!" gasped Trixi in alarm. She quickly tapped her ring and called out:

"Protect the water from the spell.
Pixie magic, please work well!"

There was a little pink flash that quickly faded away. Queen Malice sneered. "You know your magic isn't strong enough to stop mine!" she cackled.

Summer saw Trixi's bottom lip tremble. "Oh, Trixi!' she gasped. "At least you tried."

Queen Malice turned to Clearsplash Waterfall and muttered a spell under her breath, too quietly for the girls to hear.

BANG! A thunderclap exploded overhead. A black cloud burst from the end of the queen's staff and shot up into the cave at the top of the waterfall. The girls exclaimed in horror as the water started to slow. It turned from a cascade to a stream to a trickle, and then it dried up completely.

"What have you done?" Jasmine cried.

"Now no one in the Secret Kingdom will be able to get better when they're ill!" shouted Ellie.

Queen Malice smiled nastily. "Yes, and there will be no way to cure my stupid brother. He'll turn into a stink toad and then this kingdom will be mine – all mine!"

She jumped onto the back of her giant heron and with a shriek of mean laughter she flew away, her Storm Sprites flapping around her.

"Oh, no!" Trixi gasped.

A little way off, the water nymphs and snails surfaced. The snails' eye stalks were waggling wildly and many of the nymphs had started to cry.

"Please don't be upset," Summer said quickly. "We'll think of something."

"We will," Jasmine agreed. "We won't let Queen Malice get away with this."

"We'll break her spell!" Ellie said as all around the lake elves and pixies started to creep out from behind the bushes, their faces pale and worried.

"But how?" said Trixi. "Queen Malice is right, pixie magic isn't strong enough to undo her magic. And we don't even know what her spell did to stop the waterfall anyway."

"Well, we'll just have to go up to the cave and investigate," Jasmine declared.

Ellie looked up the steep cliff. "We're really going to climb all the way up there?" she gulped.

Summer shot a worried glance at her friend. She knew how much Ellie hated heights. But as she watched, Ellie lifted

her chin with determination. "Let's go!"
she said.

The three friends smiled at each other
and pulled themselves out of the water
onto the rocks at the bottom of the cliff.

But just as they looked for the best place
to start climbing, Trixi's ring started to
glow.

"Oh, my goodness!" the pixie said.

"King Merry must be sending me a message." She tapped her ring and a shower of sparks floated up into the air and formed curly golden letters in the sky:

"Dear Trixi,
Please can you magic me up a lovely deep bath? I don't know why, but I really want to be in water.
Love, King Merry."

"What am I going to do?" Trixi said, alarmed. "I'm a royal pixie, and I have to do everything I can to help the king."

"But you *are* helping him, even if he doesn't know it," said Summer. "You're helping to stop him from turning into a stink toad!"

Trixi thought for a second. "You're right." She tapped her ring and wrote a message in the air in neat pink letters.

"Dear King Merry,
I'm at Lily Pad Lake with Jasmine, Ellie
and Summer, but I'll be back soon.
Love, Trixi."

She tapped her ring again and her words vanished.

A few seconds later, a new message appeared in the sky from the king:

"Ooh, I'd love to swim in Lily Pad Lake! I'll
be with you any moment!"

"Oh dear," Trixi said. "He's coming here!"

The girls gasped. Usually they loved spending time with the kindly little king, but they couldn't let him know they what they were doing.

"But we have to go up to the cave," said Jasmine. "How will we explain that to King Merry when he doesn't know anything about the counter-potion?"

"He doesn't even know he's turning into a stink toad." Trixi scratched her head. "Maybe I can stop him coming..."

SPLASH!

Something dropped into the lake nearby, making water fly up all around them.

"King Merry!" Ellie gasped as the rosy-cheeked king bobbed up in the water. He was wearing a spotty royal-purple bathing suit and had a large yellow

rubber ring around his tubby tummy.
King Merry's shiny crown was hovering
above his curly white hair, and he still
had his half-moon spectacles perched
wonkily on his nose.

"Hello, everyone!" he cried, waving
from his rubber
ring. "I took
my rainbow
slide
straight
here.
That was
definitely
one of my
better inventions.
How lovely to see
you, girls!" He spun in a circle in the
water. "What a marvellous day for a

swim in Lily Pad Lake…*RIBBIT!*"
A loud croak burst from him.

"Oh, dearie me," the king apologised, his round cheeks blushing red. "I'm so very sorry. I still have this annoying cough and I keep making such strange noises…*RIBBIT!*"

"Don't worry at all, King Merry," said Ellie quickly.

"No, I hope your…your *cough* goes away soon," said Summer.

But the king didn't answer. "Lily pads!" he cried in delight. "Oh, I just *have* to sit on one." He splashed over towards the nearest lily pads, his arms and legs moving just like a toad's in the water.

"Poor King Merry, he's definitely getting worse," whispered Summer as the king sprang onto a lily pad.

He sighed and crouched down contentedly. "RIBBIT!" he declared.

"We must make the waterfall work again," Trixi cried. "If we don't, Aunt Maybelle won't be able to make the counter-potion and the king will turn into a stink toad forever!"

"Trixi, one of the waterfalls has disappeared," King Merry called from his lily pad. "Oh, is that why Ellie, Summer and Jasmine are here?"

"Er...yes," explained Ellie. "Queen Malice has cast some sort of spell to stop it."

"Oh, that wicked sister of mine!" wailed King Merry.

"Don't worry, King Merry," Summer said reassuringly. "We'll fix it. We're going to climb to the cave at the top and see if we can find out what's wrong with it."

"Goodness! How brave of you all." King Merry looked impressed. "I'll come too!" He jumped back into the water and swam over to them.

"Oh, no. It's okay, Your Majesty," said Jasmine hastily. "We'll be fine."

But the king wouldn't take no for an answer. "No, no, I shall come with you. The more the merrier, that's what I always say." He got out of the lake and climbed out of his rubber ring. Then he looked up at the cliff. "We have to fix that waterfall…*RIBBIT!*"

The Crystal Cave

The cliff was very steep and all the rocks
and boulders were covered in slippery
waterweed. Summer, Jasmine and Ellie
all struggled to climb up as their feet
slid on the rocks and the waterweed was
slimy under their fingers. But to the girls'
surprise, King Merry managed just fine,
nimbly hopping on his hands and feet
from one rock to another.

Trixi flew her leaf beside him nervously, but he never looked in danger of slipping.

"I don't like this!" called Ellie as they got higher and higher.

"You'll be fine," Jasmine encouraged. She and Summer were on either side of her. "Just keep going and don't look down."

"There's a handhold here," said Summer, guiding Ellie's hands. "And this rock feels safe."

Little by little the girls edged up the cliff until they reached the entrance of the cave.

"Oh wow!" Ellie gasped in wonder as she looked around. The cave was massive, as big as a cathedral, and the walls, ceiling and floor were all made out of the purest crystal. Long stalactites hung down

from the ceiling like enormous icicles.
As the light fell on them they scattered
rainbows around the white walls.

"Isn't this amazing?" breathed Summer
in awe, looking at the stalactites.

"Incredible!" agreed Jasmine.

"It's beautiful," said Trixi. "Normally all this would be underwater."

"But where has the water gone?" said King Merry, scratching his head as he looked round.

"Hmm...first we need to work out where it normally comes from," said Jasmine, thinking out loud.

They all split up to explore the cave. Ellie spotted a large rock pool near the back and went over to investigate, weaving her way past the shiny stalactites hanging down from the roof. When she got to the rock pool she saw that it was very deep and full of water. Right at the bottom of it was a large black boulder. "Hey, look at this. Over here!" she called.

The others came over.

"This must be where the water usually comes from," said Ellie, pointing at the deep pool. "But it's blocked."

"It's that big rock that's stopping the water," said Jasmine. "Queen Malice's spell must have put it there."

"Oh, my sister is so horrible," said King Merry, staring at the boulder in dismay. "Why does she always have to spoil things for everyone?"

"Well, hopefully we can sort this out," said Ellie, her mind racing. "What we need to do is move the boulder. Why don't we dive down and see if we can pull it out?"

"Okay," said Jasmine eagerly. "I don't mind trying."

"At least we can get some water for the potion," Ellie whispered, glancing at King Merry, who had gone over to look at one of the stalactites.

Trixi's forehead crinkled. "Actually, I'm not sure we can."

"What do you mean?" asked Ellie in surprise. "There's lots of water in this pool. Can't we just take some?"

In reply, Trixi swooped down near the surface of the pool on her leaf, trailing her fingers in the water. She tasted it and shook her head. "No, I'm afraid it's as I thought. Queen Malice's nasty magic has taken all the healing goodness out of the water. We need the waterfall to flow again to get fresh water that will work in the potion."

King Merry looked round curiously. "What are you whispering about?"

"Nothing, Your Majesty," said Summer hastily, going over to him. "Now, why don't you watch with me while Jasmine tries to move the boulder?"

"Oh, yes." King Merry settled himself next to Summer. "I'm not a very strong swimmer, you know," he told her.

"I always have to wear my rubber ring when I'm in the water."

Jasmine got herself ready at the side of the pool.

"It really is very deep," said Ellie, peering into the water.

Putting her arms over her head, Jasmine dived in neatly, just like she had in the swimming pool at home.

She managed to swim down, but she couldn't stay there for long. She swam back up to the surface. "I ran out of breath before I could even touch it!"

Thinking about the swimming pool gave Summer an idea. "Trixi, have you got any bubble dust? That would let us breathe underwater."

But Trixi shook her head. "I can only do the bubble dust spell at the seaside."

"Oh dear, oh dear!" King Merry paced up and down, his glasses edging down his nose. "Crowns and sceptres, what *are* we going to do?"

Jasmine smoothed her wet hair. Her tiara, thanks to Trixi's earlier spell, was still in place. "Let me try again." She climbed out and dived in once more. This time she managed to stay down for a little longer, but though she tugged and pulled, the boulder was too heavy for her to shift.

"It's no good," she said, bursting back out.

"I'll have a go!" Ellie dived in. She managed to reach the boulder, touching it with the tips of her fingers, but then she had to come back to the surface as well.

"It's too far down!" she gasped.

As Ellie stared at the boulder, there was a *plop!* in the pool next to her. Then another. She looked up as a crystal splashed into the water in front of her. "Hey!" she shouted.

Five large black shapes were zooming through the sky towards the cave entrance, their black wings flapping, their eyes gleaming meanly as they picked up

crystals from the cave floor and threw
them at the girls.

"Queen Malice's Storm Sprites!"
Summer shouted. The five Storm Sprites
swooped round the cave, dodging
between the stalactites like giant bats.

"Watch out!" cried Trixi as another
crystal rock came flying towards them.

The girls dodged away from it just in time. The Storm Sprites' laughs were echoing around the crystal cave so loudly it was hard to think.

"Oh, my goodness me!" cried King Merry, hurrying over. "Go away, you dreadful sprites!" He flapped his hands at them but the sprites ignored him.

"The waterfall is dried up forever. You'll never move that rock!" shrieked one sprite.

"Yes, we will!" shouted Ellie from the pool.

"Not with us to stop you!" the sprite yelled. He and the others dived down to pick up more of the glittering crystals.

"Stop it! Please stop it!" begged King Merry, jumping up and down in dismay, but the sprites wouldn't listen.

"Trixi, can you use your magic?" Jasmine yelled, ducking underwater as more pieces of crystal rained down into the pool.

Trixi flew on her leaf towards the sprites. She was so tiny compared to them, but she was determined. "Don't hurt my friends!" she shouted, then she tapped her ring and chanted:

"We can't avoid the rocks you throw
But this will make them very slow!"

There was a twinkle of light and each rock started moving in slow motion, as if the air around them had become thick.

Ellie giggled as the sprites howled in annoyance. The rocks travelled through the air so gradually that Trixi could knock them down before they reached the girls.

"Well done, Trixi!" the girls cheered.

"This won't last long!" she called down to them.

"Let's try again," Ellie told Jasmine. "We might be able to shift it if we work together."

Instead of going down one at a time, Ellie and Jasmine both dived down at once. Their hands tugged at the smooth dark boulder but it wasn't long before they had to come back up for air. As Summer watched anxiously, first Ellie, then Jasmine surfaced beside her, shaking their heads in disappointment.

"Can I help?" cried King Merry, coming to the edge of the pool.

"King Merry! You haven't got your rubber ring on!" Summer gasped.

But the king didn't listen. "Here I go!" he cried, and jumped straight in!

Teamwork!

"King Merry!" Jasmine, Summer and Ellie all cried as the water closed over the king's head. But the little king simply bobbed up and started swimming round like an expert. "My swimming's got much better," he declared. "I really don't know why I ever found it so hard before."

"It must be because he's turning into a stink toad," Ellie whispered to Jasmine and Summer.

"Of course!" the others realised.

"You know, I even think I could grab the boulder," called the king. "Let me see."

Turning upside down, King Merry disappeared down into the water with a kick. All three girls caught sight of his feet. They were webbed just like a toad's!

"No wonder he can swim better," exclaimed Jasmine.

The girls held their breath as King
Merry swam all the way down to the
boulder with no problem at all. He
grabbed hold of it, but although he pulled
with all his might he couldn't move it.

Suddenly a crystal splashed into the
water. "Sorry," Trixi called. "My spell's
wearing off."

"I've got an idea!" Jasmine exclaimed
suddenly. She whispered to the other
girls, then dived down and pulled at the
boulder along with King Merry.

"That's it!" Ellie cried. She jumped into
the water and pulled at Jasmine's legs.
But it still wasn't enough.

Summer looked down into the deep
pool with a gulp. She had to help!
Taking a deep breath, she closed her eyes
and dived underwater, reaching out for

Jasmine's legs too. Suddenly she felt them bump against her hands. She grabbed hold, and pulled as hard as she could. Just as she felt like she was running out of breath, the boulder came free! Clear

sparkling water gushed powerfully out of the hole the boulder had been blocking. Ellie, King Merry, Jasmine and Summer bobbed to the surface, gasping for breath. The water was already filling up the cave, lifting up all three girls and King Merry.

"We did it!" Jasmine yelled.

The girls hugged each other as the water flowed out of the pool. Soon the cave was almost full of crystal-clear water.

"It's getting very deep," Summer said nervously as she floated about.

"The current's really strong," yelled Ellie as more and more water swept through the crystal cave. Suddenly, with a gurgle like water in a bathtub, a great torrent of water spurted out of the pool!

"ARGH!" yelled the Storm Sprites as the water hit them.

"Oh my goodness!" cried Trixi, caught up in the wave too.

"Waahh!" Summer yelled. She flailed her arms and legs but Jasmine grabbed her hand.

The girls hung on tightly to each other as the water tossed them about.

Ellie fought to grab a mouthful of air. "We're going over the edge!" she shrieked in alarm.

King Merry whooped in delight as he turned somersaults while he swam. "This is fun!"

The girls held their breath as the crystal-clear water pushed them towards the edge of the cave. They were going to be swept over the edge of the waterfall!

Summer, Jasmine and Ellie yelled out loud as they tumbled down out of the cave.

"I can't look!" Ellie shouted as she spotted the lake far below. Summer reached out for the others as the water rushed and gushed all round them. But as the water poured over the edge, it magically slowed.

"Don't worry!" Trixi called. "The pixies ride the waterfalls all the time. It's completely safe."

Summer looked round as the water rushed them along gently. Even Ellie opened her eyes. It was like being on the best water slide ever!

"Whee!" shrieked Jasmine as they whooshed down.

"Look at me!" Ellie yelled, throwing her arms above her head.

King Merry croaked as he swam past happily. "RIBBIT! RIBBIT! RIBBIT!"

They splashed down into the depths
of the lake. As Summer plunged deep
underwater she felt a moment's fear, but

then hands grabbed hers. Opening her eyes, she saw Nadia's pale blue face, her long hair swirling around her. "I've got you!" Nadia's voice floated to Summer through the water.

Holding Summer's hands, she pulled her upwards, kicking powerfully. They burst through the surface of the lake and into the fresh air.

"Are you all right?" Nadia gasped anxiously.

Summer's gave an enormous grin. "I'm more than all right," she cried. "That was so much fun, I wish I could do it all over again!"

Nadia started to laugh and they hugged each other. Ellie and Jasmine were already splashing around with the water nymphs. King Merry was jumping and diving in delight. Trixi was perched on Curly's shell, smiling as her leaf dried in the sunshine. All around them on the sides of the lakes, elves and pixies were splashing in the water, cheering. The only creatures who didn't look happy were the Storm Sprites, who were dragging themselves out of the lake, their wings all bedraggled, water dripping from their pointed chins.

"Gah!" the leader cried.

"I'm all wet," said another.

"I hate water," said a third.

"Queen Malice is going to be really cross with us," said a fourth.

Looking very grumpy they all flapped away.

"We did it!" Jasmine squealed, swimming over to Summer with Ellie. "We made the waterfall flow again."

"And now everyone in the Secret Kingdom will be able to come here whenever they're unwell," said Summer happily.

Checking King Merry wasn't watching, Ellie whispered, "Now we just need to get some water for the counter-potion."

Trixi jumped onto her leaf and flew away towards the waterfall. Tapping her pixie ring, she conjured up the crystal bottle and fluttered over to the waterfall to fill it up. The water inside sparkled in the sunlight, giving out rainbows as beautiful as those in the crystal cave. Trixi zoomed back happily to the girls. "I'm going to take this to Aunt Maybelle to add to the counter-potion. I'll be back soon!"

She vanished in a pink flash of light.

Ellie grinned. "Now there are just two more ingredients to get."

Nadia and her friends came swimming over. "Come and join in our game. We're going to race the water snails!"

Soon Summer, Ellie and Jasmine were speeding round on Curly and the other water snails. Then they had a diving contest and even Summer joined in. After having to dive into the pool in the cave with Storm Sprites throwing crystals at her, it didn't feel scary at all to be diving into the beautiful warm lake. Nadia showed her how to dive really deep down and then swam with her along the bottom of the lake holding her hands as

they weaved through the waterweed and
among shoals of tiny rainbow-coloured
fish. It was wonderful!

Trixi arrived back just as the girls were
finally climbing out.

"Aunt Maybelle was really pleased," she told them, her eyes shining. "She said to say thank you. She's going to find out what the next ingredient we need is as quickly as she can. And you look like you need some towels."

Tapping her ring, she magicked up three large fluffy towels for them and then conjured a feast of lemonade fizz, freshly made cookies and strawberries.

"This has been such a fun afternoon," said Jasmine as she munched contentedly on a cookie.

"It's been brilliant!" said Ellie, draining the last of her lemonade fizz.

"I wish that the Secret Kingdom could always be this happy." Summer sighed, waving to King Merry who was still swimming contentedly in the lake.

Trixi nodded worriedly as King Merry dived under the water, kicking up his webbed feet as he went. "We must find the last two ingredients as quickly as we can. Time's running out – King Merry's in terrible danger."

Ellie looked at the king as he surfaced. "We can't let him turn into a stink toad," she whispered.

"As soon as you know what the next ingredient is, call us and we'll come and help straight away," Jasmine said to Trixi.

"I will. I promise," said Trixi, her blue eyes wide.

The girls stood up. "Bye!" Summer called to Nadia and the other water nymphs. "It was great to meet you!"

"Goodbye!" They all waved.

Summer, Ellie and Jasmine took hold of

one another's hands.

"Goodbye for now," said Trixi, kissing each of them on the tip of their nose, and then she tapped her ring. There was a flash of pink light and the girls felt themselves being carried away in a magical whirlwind.

They landed back inside the tiny changing cubicle at the swimming pool. The Magic Box was on the bench beside them, not glowing any more.

"We're home!" said Summer, looking round.

"Until the Secret Kingdom needs us again," said Jasmine, carefully wrapping up the box and giving it to Ellie to look after. "Should we go back in the swimming pool for a little bit?"

"Definitely," said Ellie, linking arms

with her. "I want to do some more
diving."

"I do too," said Jasmine. They both
looked at Summer.

"Oh, yes, diving's fun!" Summer joined
them. She dropped her voice to a whisper.
"Well, as long as there aren't any Storm
Sprites around!"

Giggling together, the three girls headed
to the pool.

In the next Secret Kingdom adventure, Ellie, Summer and Jasmine visit

Fairytale Forest

Read on for a sneak peek...

Books! Books! Books!

Summer Hammond ran her finger slowly along the spines of the books on the library shelf. There were so many books with so many stories in! She pushed her long blonde plaits back over her shoulders and felt happiness run through her as she tried to decide which book to pick. She loved reading and the library was one of her favourite places to go. So when Ellie Macdonald, one of her best friends, had said she needed to come and find a book for her art project, Summer had been eager to come with her, and they'd dragged their other best friend, Jasmine Smith, along as well!

Ellie was looking through a big art book all about making puppets. "This book is just what I need for my school project," she said in a low voice so the librarian wouldn't tell them off for talking. "I'm going to sit down and make some notes."

Jasmine sat down next to her. "How long will you be?" She sighed.

"I'm not sure," Ellie replied.

"Why don't you come and choose a

book while we wait?" Summer said to Jasmine.

But Jasmine shook her head. "No. I'll just sit here. I'm not really keen on reading."

Summer knew Jasmine much preferred singing and dancing and being active to reading quietly. But surely there was a book her friend would like? There had to be!

She started looking on the shelves. There! She spotted the perfect book. "Try this one!" She took it off the shelf and carried it over.

Jasmine read the title. "*Pandora Parks: Pop Star!*" The girl on the cover looked quite like her, with long dark hair and brown eyes. She was holding a microphone and was dressed in a red catsuit. Jasmine turned it over to read the description on the back cover. "Actually, this book does look quite good," she admitted.

"Try reading it," Summer encouraged her. "There's a whole series of books about Pandora. She's a pop star in one book, an actress in another, and then a model, and she has loads of adventures. I bet you'll like them and..." Summer grinned as she realised that Jasmine was already turning over the first page. Summer smiled to herself and then went back to the shelf. Now, which book was she going to read?

She pulled out several books before she decided on an animal rescue story. She sat down with the others and began reading.

After about half an hour, Ellie shut her notebook. "Okay, I've got all the notes I need for my school project. Now I just need to go home and actually make the puppet!" She stood up and put the book back on the shelf.

Summer stretched and got to her feet too. She looked over to where Jasmine still had her head buried in *Pandora Parks: Pop Star!* "Jasmine, we're going back to Ellie's house."

Jasmine blinked. "But I'm at a really exciting bit. I can't stop reading now!"

Summer chuckled. "So, maybe you're keen on reading *some* books then?"

"Definitely this one. It's amazing!" enthused Jasmine. "I'll have to borrow it from the library so I can finish it. Pandora has so many adventures!"

Ellie overheard. "Like us!"

The three friends grinned at each other. They shared a very special secret. At their school jumble sale they had found an old carved wooden box. It had turned out to be a magic box made by King Merry, who ruled an enchanted land called the Secret Kingdom. Whenever the people of the Secret Kingdom needed the girls' help their pixie friend, Trixibelle, would send them a message in the box, then whisk them away to the wonderful land.

"Where's the Magic Box now?" whispered Jasmine.

"Here," said Ellie, putting her bag on the table and patting it.

"I wonder when we'll get another message from the Secret Kingdom?" Summer said.

Ellie opened the top of her bag and took the Magic Box out. Its wooden sides were carved with magical creatures and its lid was studded with six green gems. "Oh, I wish it would glow!" she said longingly.

A bright light flashed across the mirrored lid of the box.

"It worked!" Ellie exclaimed in astonishment.

Jasmine looked hopefully at the box. "I wish I had a million pounds!"

"Ssh!" the librarian scolded from her desk.

"Come on!" said Ellie, pushing the box back into her bag. Her eyes sparkled with excitement. "The Secret Kingdom needs us! We'd better find somewhere more private where we can look at the box properly and see if it has a message for us."

"Follow me!" Heart pounding, Summer led the way out of the children's section and down the aisles. Another adventure was starting! "I wonder where in the Secret Kingdom we'll have to go this time!" she whispered.

"And what ingredient we'll be trying to find!" said Jasmine.

The Secret Kingdom was in real trouble. King Merry's sister, evil Queen Malice, had given him a cake with a potion inside. He was now slowly turning into a horrible creature called a stink toad. Queen Malice planned to take over the kingdom when the transformation was complete. The only way to stop the curse was to give King Merry a magical counter-potion, but to make it they needed six very rare ingredients. So far, they had collected bubblebee honeycomb, silverspun sugar, dream dust and some healing water from Clearsplash Waterfall. There were just two ingredients left to get!

They reached the far corner of the library, which was full of volumes of dusty old leather-bound journals. "We should be safe here," Summer whispered. "No one ever comes down this aisle."

The girls knelt down and took out the Magic Box from Ellie's bag. Its mirrored lid was still shining brightly with a silver light. The girls watched as curly letters appeared and formed into words. Jasmine read them out:

"Ellie, Summer, Jasmine, please,
Look for somewhere that has trees.
Find the place where tales all grow.
That is where you have to go!"

As she finished speaking, sparkles
rippled across the surface of the box and
the lid magically sprang open. Inside
the box there were six compartments,
each containing a different magic object.
One of them was a beautiful map of the
Secret Kingdom, which now floated out
and opened itself up in front of the girls'
eyes.

Read
*Fairytale
Forest*
to find out what
happens next!

Secret Kingdom

Bubble Volcano
ROSIE BANKS

Sugarsweet Bakery
ROSIE BANKS

Dream Dale
ROSIE BANKS

Lily Pad Lake
ROSIE BANKS

Midnight Maze
ROSIE BANKS

Fairytale Forest
ROSIE BANKS

Series 2

Wicked Queen Malice has cast a spell to turn King Merry into a toad! Can the girls find six magic ingredients to save him?

Secret Kingdom

Be in on the secret.
Collect them all!

Enchanted Palace
ROSIE BANKS

Unicorn Valley
ROSIE BANKS

Cloud Island
ROSIE BANKS

Mermaid Reef
ROSIE BANKS

Magic Mountain
ROSIE BANKS

Glitter Beach
ROSIE BANKS

Series 1

When Jasmine, Summer and Ellie discover
the magical land of the Secret Kingdom,
a whole world of adventure awaits!

Secret Kingdom

Catch up on the very first
books in the beautiful
Secret Kingdom treasury!

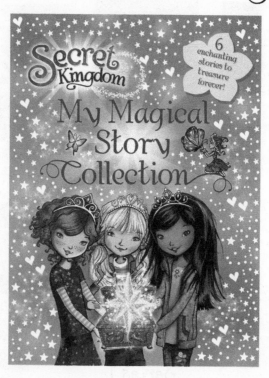